The Big Apple Mystery

by Peter Maloney
and Felicia Zekauskas

SCHOLASTIC INC.

New York Toronto London Auckland Sydney
Mexico City New Delhi Hong Kong Buenos Aires

To Christine, Amanda, and
all the wonderful people at
the Washington Market School
in Tribeca

ISBN 0-439-67638-X

12 11 10 9 8 7 6 5 4 3   8 9/0

Printed in the U.S.A.
First printing, October 2004

CHAPTER 1
Class Trip

The day of the class trip finally arrived.

"All aboard!" cried Mrs. Robinson.

The children piled into the bright yellow school bus.

Soon they were off.
They were on their way.
They were going. . .

"Now, remember," said Mrs. Robinson,
"never lose sight of your buddy.
And when I ring this bell, everyone
return to the school bus."

"Peter, you're with Felicia.

"Russell, you're with Tobi.

"Rich, you're with Cliff.

"And Lew, you're with Patty."

9

CHAPTER 2
Picky, Picky

The orchard was filled with ripe apples.

There were red ones,
yellow ones,
and green ones.

There were even a few rotten ones.

"Taste this apple," Felicia said
to Peter.

Peter took a bite.
The apple was crisp,
sweet, and juicy.

"It's delicious!" said Peter.

"Wrong!" laughed Felicia. "It's a McIntosh!"

CHAPTER 3
Where's Peter?

Soon everybody's bag was
filled with apples.
Then Mrs. Robinson rang
the bell.

"We better go," Felicia said to Peter.
"It's time to meet at the bus."
But Peter didn't answer.

Peter hadn't heard her.
Peter was gone.

"Oh, no!" cried Felicia. "Peter's lost.
I better get help."

CHAPTER 4
Here! Here! Not Here!

Back at the bus, Mrs. Robinson was
taking attendance.
"Russell?" she called.

"Here!"

"Tobi?"

"Here!"

"Felicia?"
There was a moment of silence.
Then Felicia suddenly appeared.
She was out of breath.

"Peter's missing!" she gasped.

"Felicia, what happened?" asked Mrs. Robinson. "Peter is your buddy."

"I don't know," said Felicia. "I turned around for a second and he was gone!"

"Everybody get on the bus," said Mrs. Robinson. "Felicia and Russell, come with me. We're going to find Peter!"

CHAPTER 5
The Giant Apple

Felicia, Russ Deluca, and Mrs.
Robinson went back into the orchard.

"We were right here," explained
Felicia. "Then the bell rang and
Peter was gone!"

They went from tree to tree,
but Peter wasn't anywhere.
Then Felicia looked up.

"Look! Up in that tree!" cried
Russ Deluca. "It's a giant red apple."

"It's red, all right," said Felicia.
"But that's no apple. That's Peter!"

"Peter! What are you doing up there?"
called Mrs. Robinson.

"I climbed up to pick an apple, but then I was afraid to climb down," said Peter.

"How are we going to get him down?" asked Felicia.

"Let's shake the tree," said Russ Deluca. "That will get him down!"

"Russell, run and get Farmer Brown," said Mrs. Robinson. "And ask him to bring a ladder."

CHAPTER 6

Plop! Plop! Help!

Mrs. Robinson and Felicia waited
under the tree.
Suddenly, a strong wind blew.
Branches swayed.
Leaves flew.
Dozens of apples plopped to the
ground.
So did two red sneakers!

"I'm losing my grip!" cried Peter.
Just then Farmer Brown and
Russ Deluca came running.
They leaned the ladder against
the tree.

Farmer Brown climbed up and
plucked Peter and the big apple from
the branch.

Peter was safe.

"Well!" said Mrs. Robinson. "I guess you win the prize for the biggest apple of the day."

Peter's cheeks turned bright red.

"Look!" teased Russ Deluca. "Peter's blushing!"

"Peter's not blushing," said Felicia. "He's ripening!"